MORE
TALES OF
AMANDA PIG

Jean Van Leeuwen
PICTURES BY
ANN SCHWENINGER

DIAL BOOKS FOR YOUNG READERS
NEW YORK

85 B96 30

Published by
Dial Books for Young Readers
A Division of E. P. Dutton
2 Park Avenue
New York, New York 10016

Published simultaneously in Canada by
Fitzhenry & Whiteside Limited, Toronto

8.89
0.1

Printed in Hong Kong by South China Printing Co.

The Dial Easy-to-Read logo is a trademark of
Dial Books for Young Readers
A division of E. P. Dutton ® TM 1,162,718

Library of Congress Cataloging in Publication Data
Van Leeuwen, Jean. More tales of Amanda pig.
Summary: Five more adventures of Amanda Pig and her family
in which noisy cousins come to visit and Father
gets a stuffed toy for his birthday.
1. Children's stories, American.
[1. Pigs—Fiction. 2. Family life—Fiction.]
I. Schweninger, Ann, ill. II. Title.
PZ7.V3273MI 1985   [E]   84-28775
ISBN 0-8037-0223-X   ISBN 0-8037-0224-8 (lib. bdg.)

First Edition
COBE
10 9 8 7 6 5 4 3 2 1

The full-color artwork was prepared using carbon pencil,
colored pencils, and watercolor washes. It was then camera-separated
and reproduced as red, blue, yellow, and black halftones.

Reading Level 1.9

For Elizabeth
who, when she grows up,
will never ever eat eggs

J.V.L.

For Anne Schwartz
and Atha Tehon

A.S.

CONTENTS

MOTHER AND FATHER

"Father," said Amanda.

"What is it?" asked Father.

"I'm talking to Oliver," said Amanda.

"He is the father.

You are the grandfather."

"I see," said Father.

"Father," said Amanda,

"our baby is hungry

and there is no food in the house.

Will you go to the store?"

"Yes, Mother," said Oliver.

"What did you say?" asked Mother.

"I'm talking to Amanda," said Oliver.

"You are the grandmother."

Oliver came back

with a big bag of food.

"Our baby keeps crying," said Amanda.

"I think she has a temperature.

Will you hold her, Father?"

Amanda gave Oliver the baby.

Oliver gave Amanda the bag of food.

She dropped it on the floor.

"Oh, dear," she said.

"Now we have to sweep the floor."

Oliver and Amanda swept the floor.

"Amanda, I mean Mother,"
said Oliver. "I think I hear
the other babies crying."

"What other babies?" asked Amanda.

"Our other babies," said Oliver.

"I will go check."

He came back with the other babies.

"They are all sick," he said.

"They have a hundred and two."

"Oh, dear," said Amanda.

"I better call the doctor."

"Yes, Doctor," she said.

"I will give them the pink medicine.

I have to hang up now.

The spaghetti and meatballs

are burning on the stove."

Amanda hung up.

"Oh, dear," she said.

"Our dinner is all burned up."

"Never mind," said Oliver.

"I will cook banana pancakes."

Amanda gave the babies
the pink medicine.
"I think they are feeling better."
she said.

"Dinner is ready," said Oliver.

Oliver and Amanda and all the babies sat down at the table.

"Don't talk with your mouth full, Sallie Rabbit," said Amanda.

"Tiger, stop throwing food
at Elephant," said Oliver.
"These babies have no manners
at all," said Amanda. "Oh, dear.
Now look what Sallie Rabbit did."
"What did she do?" asked Oliver.
"Spilled her milk," said Amanda.
"All over everything."

"We better get the mop," said Oliver.

They went to the kitchen.

"Grandmother," said Amanda.

"May we have juice and cookies?

We are all tired out."

"It's the babies," said Oliver.

"How many babies do you have?"

asked Mother.

"Twelve," said Amanda.

"You better sit down and rest,"

said Mother.

Oliver and Amanda rested.

Mother got the juice and cookies.

"Being a mother and father

is hard work," said Amanda.

"It certainly is," said Mother.

"Mother," said Oliver.

"Do you hear a baby crying?"

Amanda listened.

She took another bite of cookie.

"I don't hear a thing," she said.

COMPANY

"Why are you cooking and cooking?" asked Amanda.

"Company is coming," said Mother.

"Who is the company?" asked Amanda.

"Your aunt Sara and uncle Mort,"

said Mother. "And your cousins

Sam and Emily and Peter."

Oliver put on his sailor suit.

Amanda put on her sundress.

She dressed Sallie Rabbit

in her best pajamas.

They waited for the company.

"When will they come?" asked Oliver.

"Any minute," said Mother.

"Is it any minute yet?" asked Amanda.

"Here they are," said Father.

Uncle Mort lifted Amanda up high.

"Who is this big girl?" he asked.

"Amanda," said Amanda.

Mother and Father

and Aunt Sara and Uncle Mort

sat down in the living room.

The cousins went outside.

"What is there to do?" asked Sam.

"Play in my sandbox," said Amanda.

"Sandboxes are for babies," said Sam.

"Play in my fort," said Oliver.

All the cousins went to Oliver's fort.

Amanda built a sand castle alone.

"What can we ride?" asked Sam.

"I have a wagon," said Amanda.

"I have a new bike," said Oliver.

"Oh, boy," said Sam. "Let's ride it."

He zoomed all over the yard

on Oliver's bike.

After his turn everyone had a turn.

Except Amanda.

Her feet didn't reach the pedals.

Then they played hide-and-seek.

Sam found Oliver

hiding in the apple tree.

Oliver found Emily

hiding in the sandbox.

No one even looked for Amanda.

"Lunch time!" called Mother.
Everyone ran to the picnic table
under the apple tree.

"Oh, boy, lemonade!" said Sam.

"And chocolate cake!" said Oliver.

They pushed and grabbed and laughed.

"This company is too noisy,"
said Amanda.
She took Sallie Rabbit
and crawled under the table.

It was dark there.
And quiet.
And there were a lot of feet.
"It's like a little house,"
said Amanda.

"It's a cave," said someone.

It was her cousin Peter.

"We could pretend

it's a cave house," said Amanda.

"We could," said Peter.

"I have a rabbit," said Amanda.

"Her name is Sallie Rabbit."

"I have an alligator," said Peter.

"His name is Alligator."

Then Amanda and Peter had a picnic

in their cave house.

They ate chocolate cake

and listened to the noisy company

and counted feet

and picked up cake crumbs.

And Sallie Rabbit and Alligator

ate every one.

THE BUBBLE BATH

"Just look at you, Sallie Rabbit,"
said Amanda.
"You've got egg on your chin
and grape ice pop on your paws
and mud on your stomach.
What a mess."

"Tiger has four stripes

on his stomach," said Oliver.

"And seven spots."

"What these babies need is a bath,"

said Amanda.

Oliver ran water in the bathtub.

Amanda poured in some bubble bath.

"Okay, Sallie Rabbit," she said.

"Start scrubbing. I will help you."

Amanda worked on Sallie's stomach.

She scrubbed and scrubbed.

"Sorry, Sallie," she said.

"This is hard dirt. We need more soap."

She poured in some shampoo.

"I can't get the bubble gum
out of Tiger's tail," said Oliver.
He poured in more bubble bath.

"Oops!" He dropped in
the whole bottle by mistake.
"Oh, well," said Amanda.
"Our babies will get really clean."

Bubbles rose in the air.

Bubbles spilled over the bathtub
and covered the floor.

"Uh-oh," said Amanda.

She couldn't see Sallie Rabbit.

She couldn't even see the bathtub.

Bubbles were creeping out the door
and into the hall.

"Help!" called Amanda.

Mother came upstairs.

"Amanda! Oliver! Where are you?"

"Here," said Amanda.

"In all these bubbles."

"What should we do?" asked Oliver.

"Let the water out of the tub,"
said Mother.

"I can't find the tub," said Oliver.

"I'll do it," said Mother.

But she slipped and slid

and landed on the floor.

"Ouch!" cried Oliver.

"You just found me."

"And me," said Amanda.

Slowly the bubbles started to melt.

Amanda could see the bathtub again.

And Mother's face.

It was angry.

"Just look at this mess," she said.

"How could you make such a mess?

And look at you."

Amanda looked at Oliver.

"You look like a clown," she said.

"You look like a cloud," said Oliver.

"And look at Mother.

She looks like she is wearing a hat."

They looked in the mirror.

Mother laughed.

"I like my new hat," she said.

"I like my new nose," said Oliver.

They all laughed.

Then they started cleaning up.

Oliver and Amanda wrapped

Sallie Rabbit and Tiger in towels.

"Look, Mother," said Amanda.

"Our babies are clean."

"So they are," said Mother.

"But no more bubble baths for a while."

Amanda blew a bubble

out of Sallie Rabbit's ear.

"Did you hear that, Sallie?"

she said. "No more bubble baths."

THE BIRTHDAY PRESENT

"Today is somebody's birthday,"
said Mother.

"Is it my birthday?" asked Amanda.

"No," said Mother.

"You just had your birthday."

"I want it to be my birthday again,"
said Amanda.

"So I can get bigger and bigger."

"It's not my birthday," said Oliver.

"No," said Mother. "Yours is soon,
but today is Father's birthday."

"Let's have a party," said Amanda.

"Good idea," said Mother.

"What shall we have for the party?"

"Birthday cake," said Amanda.

"Ice cream," said Oliver.

"Balloons," said Amanda.

"Party hats," said Oliver.

"And a present," said Mother.

She took a box out of the closet.

Oliver and Amanda looked inside.

"Father doesn't wear short pants,"
said Oliver.

"It's a bathing suit," said Mother.

"I want to give Father a present,"
said Oliver. "But I can't buy one."

"Me too," said Amanda.

"A present doesn't need to be
something you buy," said Mother.
"It can be anything at all
that you think Father would like."
Oliver went to his room.

"Father would like this," he said.
"It is a very round rock."
"What a nice present," said Mother.
"I will help you wrap it up."

Amanda went to her room.

She looked at all her toys.

"Father is too big for blocks,"

she said. "And he has his own car.

What could be a present for Father?"

She saw Sallie Rabbit

sitting on her bed.

"If I were Father," she said,
"this is what I would like
for my birthday."
She picked her up.
"But I like Sallie too," she said.

She put her down.
"But it would be the very best
birthday present," she said.

Father liked his birthday party.

He liked all his presents.

"Something to wear

and something to hold

and something to hug," he said.

"Thank you, everyone."

Later Amanda lay in her bed.

She couldn't sleep.

Her bed felt wide and empty

without Sallie Rabbit.

Father opened the door.

"Amanda," he said. "I can't sleep.

It's Sallie Rabbit.

She keeps wiggling."

"She never wiggles when she sleeps with me," said Amanda.

"Maybe she misses you," said Father.

"Well, I am her mother," said Amanda.

"I think she still needs a mother," said Father.

"Would you mind

taking care of her for me

until she is a little bigger?"

"I wouldn't mind," said Amanda.

"Thank you," said Father.

Amanda hugged Sallie Rabbit tight.

"Good night, Father," she said.

"Good night, Sallie Rabbit."

GROWING UP

"Mother," said Amanda.

"What can I help you do?"

"You can help mix up these muffins for dinner," said Mother.

Amanda helped mix up the muffins.

"What a good helper

you are getting to be," said Mother.

"I can do a lot of things,"

said Amanda.

"I am almost grown up, you know.

Soon I will be moving out."

"Oh, my," said Mother. "Already?

Come and tell me about it
while we wait for Father and Oliver."
Mother and Amanda sat
in the big chair.
"What do you think you will do
when you grow up?" asked Mother.
"I will be a ballet dancer,"
said Amanda. "And a cook
and a doctor
and I will fly to the moon."

"All at once?" said Mother.

"You will be busy."

"I am going to be very busy

when I grow up," said Amanda.

"Where will you live," asked Mother,

"when you are not on the moon?"

"I will build a house

next door to you," said Amanda.

"And I will do whatever I want
whenever I want to do it.
I will wear perfume all the time
and go to bed at midnight
and never eat eggs."
"That sounds good," said Mother.
"Will you have any babies?"
"Maybe six," said Amanda.

"I wonder what I will look like
when I grow up.
Will I look like you?"
"Maybe," said Mother.
"But mostly I think you will look
just like yourself.
And I will miss you."
"Don't worry," said Amanda.
"I will still come to see you.
On Mondays and Fridays."

"That will be good," said Mother.

"Will we still sit in the big chair?"

"I don't think so," said Amanda.

"I think I will be too big to fit."

"Oh, dear," said Mother.

"I will really miss that.

We had better hug now

before it is too late."

They had a big hug.

"Mother," said Amanda.

"Maybe I won't get so very big
when I grow up.

Maybe we will still fit."

"I hope so," said Mother.

And they had another big hug

in the big chair

waiting for Father and Oliver.